I0663387

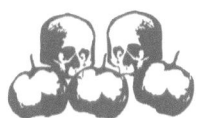

CRITICAL PRAISE FOR HAROLD JAFFE

Books by Harold Jaffe

Strange Fruit

& Other Plays

Harold Jaffe

Black Scat Books
2021

ISBN 978-1-7373711-5-1

Cover photograph: Jurien Huggins
Cover design: N. Conquest

ACKNOWLEDGMENTS:

—*Salaam* and portions of *Death in Texas* were read in a theater on Jane St near the Hudson in NYC. in the winter of 2015.
—*Salaam* was performed by students in San Diego at SDSU in the Spring of 2016.
—*Salaam* was performed at a bookstore in La Jolla in Spring 2017.
—*Manson* was read in NYC in a cafe on 3rd Street and Second Avenue in the Spring of 2018.
—*Artaud / Bataille* were performed in a small theater on Bleecker St. (NYC) in Fall, 2019.
—An early version of *Strange Fruit* was read in San Diego at SDSU.
—Early versions of *Bud & Norma Jeane* and *Jimi/Janis/JM* were read at a book-store-cafe in LA in Fall 2019.
—*Death in Texas* was performed for a week run in a small theater in San Diego in Winter 2019.

BLACK SCAT BOOKS
publishers of sublime art & literature
BlackScatBooks.com

Contents

STRANGE FRUIT

PLAYERS

Billie Holiday (Lady Day)
Lester Young (Prez)
Bobby Tucker (Billie's piano accompanist)

Village Vanguard, jazz club in Greenwich Village, after a gig with Billie Holiday and Lester Young in 1941.

Lady Day has left as have the two sidemen, bass and drums.

Lady's close friend Prez and her accompanist Bobby Tucker are chatting by the piano. Prez is cleaning the reeds and mouthpiece of his sax.

Strange Fruit
Southern trees bear a strange fruit
Blood on the leaves and blood at the root
Black body swinging in the southern breeze
Strange fruit hanging from the poplar trees
Pastoral scene of the gallant south
The bulging eyes and the twisted mouth
Scent of magnolia sweet and fresh
And the sudden smell of burning flesh
Here is a fruit for the crows to pluck
For the rain to gather, for the wind to suck
For the sun to rot, for a tree to drop
Here is a strange and bitter crop.

TUCKER

Man, you heard that, Prez?

Honky bartender jingling his cash register real loud when Billie was into "Strange Fruit."

PREZ

I heard it.

TUCKER

Nobody could hear Billie good.

She was all broke up about it.

Honky still here cleanin up.

There behind the bar.

I feel like like cleanin his ass up, Prez.

I mean it.

PREZ

Ain't the first time.

Every time I gig with Lady and she sing that lyric, same kinda shit.

White folks acting Jim Crow on her.

TUCKER

Guess some white folks just like lynchin Negroes.

PREZ

Damn sure do it enough.

TUCKER

But ain't this Greenwich Village where white folks is so-called liberal?

PREZ

They liberal compared to other whites, maybe.

But what do that mean?

TUCKER

And they say a white guy wrote the song.

A Jew.

PREZ

Shit, Jews—they only half step 'bove Negroes in this country.

TUCKER

He's a school teacher in the Bronx somewhere.

Jew that wrote "Strange Fruit."

He sposed to be a Red. A Communist.

PREZ

Good for him.

TUCKER

He's a high school history teacher's what I heard

Guess he's read some real history.

PREZ

Yeah, real.

American history I read is fulla horse shit.

Not just about Negroes.

Indians too. American Indians.

Man, how they been fucked over.

TUCKER
[Joking]
You readin history, Prez?

Thought you busy blowin your horn.

No cat blow like you gone spend time reading so-called

American history.

PREZ

Back in Mississippi when I was a lil bitty black chile.

Didn't take much readin to see how shit stink.

TUCKER

I heard that this Jewish history teacher cat approached Billie

after a gig at Café Society.

He handed her the lyric—Strange Fruit—printed on a sheet of paper.

She read it on the spot and wept.

Prez, I jus hate to see Billie all broke up with that lyric.

Maybe she jus shouldn't sing it no more.

PREZ

It's a lyric that gotten real close to her like you said.

TUCKER

Tomorrow night we gone do it all over again, Prez.

I'm thinkin to bring my '38.
That honky do his jinglin' shit to drown Billie out I'll kill his ass.

I ain lyin.

PREZ

Once you get to shootin white folks it gone be hard to stop, Tuck.

TUCKER

You're right.

Dint think of that.

PREZ

Looka here, Lady's back.

[Billie Holiday has come back in the club through a back exit]

TUCKER

What up, Billie?

LADY

Misplaced my keys.

Musta left 'em here somewhere.

You see them around, fellas?

Mister's getting real hungry.

TUCKER

Mister's a big Boxer dog, Billie.

I guess he can wait a bit.

How come Mister wasn't here with you?

Listenin and watchin real close like usual.

LADY

I dint bring him cause if he seen what that bartender
done he'd kill im.

When I'm broke up Mister's real broke up.

And I kinda lost it at the end with "Strange Fruit."

Got all turned around.

TUCKER

Yeah, me and Prez just talkin 'bout that, Billie.

You sing that lyric great, but, damn, it take a lot outta you.

LADY

John Hammond won't let me record it on Columbia.

Says it will ruin my career.

PREZ

That what he says?

TUCKER

Damn honky talk.

He's a scared shit rich white man producer is all.

You can record it on Commodore, Billie.

Commodore loves your work.

LADY

That hurt bad what Hammond told me.

Surprised me, y'know.

TUCKER

Nothin white folks do gone surprise me.

Specially if they rich like Hammond.

That fool think he owns you.

And folks call him civil rights activist.

PREZ

He call hisself civil rights activist.

TUCKER

Wasn't his mama part of that billionaire Vanderbilt family?

Lynchers theirselves probly.

[Pause]

LADY

What you think I oughta do, Prez?

PREZ

I'm with Tuck.

There a dozen labels love to have you.

TUCKER

Or you could stop singin that lyric, Billie.

It take a whole lot outta you.

[Bartender shouts: Hurry up, closing!]

LADY

I got to find them keys, fellas.

Mister's been in there all alone.

TUCKER

We'll look for your keys, Billie.

They closin', so we gotta look fast.

Was they in your purse or what?

LADY

I think so.

But they ain't there.

That bartender noise got me turned around.

I felt messed up even in the taxi.

Hope I dint leave em in the taxi.

PREZ

I found your keys, Lady.

They was on the floor to the side of the exit.

TUCKER

When you pushed open the door you musta dropped em.

LADY

Thanks a lot, fellas.

I oughta make up an extra key for you, Prez.

Maybe you too, Tuck.

This shit got me all turned around.

TUCKER

I'm gonna talk to this piece a shit honky right now.

LADY

Don't Tuck, please.

I don't care about him.

Gotta hold myself together.

Tomorrow Mister will be with me listenin real close.

[Following night is Friday, the Village Vanguard is filled with jazz fans. Lady Day and Prez are finishing their set for the night.

Mister, Lady's big boxer, unleashed, is just off-stage looking, listening.

Lady is obviously preoccupied, as is Bobby Tucker at the piano, but Prez is blowing great as always: airy, introspective, economical, subtly passionate.

Winding up with "Strange Fruit," the bartender jingles the cash register very loud. Lady stops singing and immediately Mister bounds into the club, leaps onto the bar scattering patrons and drinks, and is all over the bartender who falls on his back.

Lady herself has to pull Mister off.

The bartender is bleeding from his face.

The bartender suffers deep bite wounds on the face and throat but recovers.

When he threatens to sue Billie Holiday, the Village Vanguard owner steps in, pays him off then fires him, preferring to keep

Lady Day and Lester Young for two more weeks to admiring customers and consistently good reviews.

But the "Jim Crow" interventions when Lady sings "Strange Fruit" continue.]

SPLISH SPLASH

PLAYERS
Joan
Jon

Stage is empty but for a bed and a door, behind which is a bathtub.

JON

[Knocks softly at the bathroom door]
Are you still in the bath?

JOAN
What do you want?

JON
Are you still having your bath?

JOAN
Why?

JON
Why?
[Joking]
Because we're a team.

A team knows what each other is doing.

JOAN
Does "team" mean you follow my every move?

JON
I'm not following your every move, Joan.
I'm just asking an innocent question.

JOAN
When was the last time you asked an innocent question?

JON
What does that supposed to mean?

JOAN
Okay, I'm still in the bath.
Put your ear to the door and listen to me splash.

[splash splash]

JON
"Splish, splash, I was takin' a bath
Round about a Saturday night . . . "
Do you remember the Bobby Darin song?

JOAN
No, I don't remember the Bobby Darin song.

JON
He recorded it in the late '50s.

Made him a star.

He didn't live very long.

Heart condition.

JOAN

Of course I remember Bobby Darin!

He abused Sandra Dee, his wife.

JON

What?

I never heard that.

Where'd you hear that rumor?

JOAN

CNN or MSNBC, probably both.

JON

They're both long dead, Bobby Darin and Sandra Dee.

JOAN

That doesn't mean he didn't abuse her while they were married.

So that's Bobby Darin.

What else do you have up your sleeve?

JON

I don't have anything else up my sleeve.

[Pause]

I hope you haven't been drinking again.

JOAN

No, I haven't been drinking.

I was simply having a nice bath with that nice soap I bought at Nordstrom online, then you start interrogating me.

JON
No goblet of Pinot Grigio by the bathtub?

JOAN
Fuck you, Jon.

JON
Look, I was kidding.

[Pause]

Can I join you?

JOAN
What?

JON
Can I join you in the bath?

JOAN
Now?

JON
Yes, now.

We are lovers, remember?

We've had a few baths together.

JOAN
In our old apartment where the tub was large.

In this new place the tub is small.

You're six-feet-four, dude.

JON

I'm 6-2-and-a-half, but never mind.

JOAN

Anyway, I seem to have used all the hot water.

I'm getting out.

JON

Sorry I interrupted your bath, Joan.

JOAN

Forget it

JON

Do you want me to dry you?

JOAN

Huh?

Well okay.

Get the large beach towel from the towel closet.

JON

Okay.

[Later. In bed, apres sex]

JON

You smell nice.

JOAN

It's that soap from Nordstrom.

JON

Did you enjoy that?

JOAN

What?

JON

Making love.

You had a violent orgasm.

JOAN

I wouldn't call it violent.

JON

What would you call it?

JOAN

I don't know, Jon.

Is this more interrogation?

JON

No, it's a man talking to his lover.

Why are you so edgy?

JOAN

I am what I am.

Sorry you don't approve.

JON

I hope I'm wrong, but I'm guessing you've bought in to the hate white males gospel that's making the rounds.

I thought you were above that.

JOAN

Above what exactly?

JON

Above the lunacy of this new McCarthyism.

Every white hetero male is guilty until proven innocent.

JOAN

Is that what I'm doing?

JON

I don't know.

You tell me.

JOAN

I'm expressing some independent thinking.

The fact that we live together and have sex doesn't mean I'm enslaved to you.

JON

Enslaved!

I don't know how to respond except to say that you've contracted the contagion.

JOAN

I don't know what that means except that it's an insult.

We live together because it is impossibly expensive for working people to afford rent.

JON

Really?

So our being together for nearly a year is simply a matter of convenience?

JOAN

Convenience is a factor, yes.

We're in crazily expensive San Francisco, remember?

JON

So there is no love in our relationship?

It is simply convenience with occasional sex?

JOAN

Maybe there would be something like love if you'd stop interrogating me.

JON

Interrogating again!

Where the fuck did you pick that up?

JOAN

Now you're saying I can't think for myself?

JON

Just an observation, Joan.

You seem to forget how good you felt almost immediately after feeling good.

JOAN

Feeling good doesn't mean being enslaved.

JON

How am I enslaving you, Joan?

JOAN

You push me when I want some alone time in my bath.

And when we have sex you make a big deal about it.

Sex is sex, Jon.

If it wasn't me you'd be fucking someone else.

If it wasn't you I'd be fucking someone else, right?

JON

That's cold.

I never heard you talk like that.

JOAN

I'm not that old, Jon.

I'm still learning things, like how white hetero men have treated women.

Have treated people.

JON

What does that mean?

Going back 60 years when the body was open?

Persecuting a man for allegedly acting inappropriately with a female?

When both the male and female are long dead?

Bobby Darin and Sandra Dee were married in the early Sixties.

JOAN

Abuse is abuse is abuse, Jon.

[Pause]

JON

This "new normal" of females surrounded by razor wire is not normal, Joan.

The old normal in 1965 for example of the body being open and not paranoid is way less neurotic than what's going on with #Metoo.

JOAN

I disagree.

White men have fucked over the world, and especially women.

Now it is payback time.

If there are some small excesses now and again they are excusable given the crimes that were committed.

JON

Is it a crime to have touched a woman's bare back 60 years ago?

Or to have said to a woman friend: You look sexy?

Women were doing and saying the same things to their male friends.

How far back do you go with this new normal?

Is there no statute of limitations?

JOAN

No, there isn't.

JON

You were not born until much later.

All you know of the Sixties and early Seventies are the self-serving pieties you see on the Internet and on TV.

JOAN
You weren't born then either.

JON
No, but I've read widely about the period.

JOAN
Right. You have a Ph.D.

My bad.

I'm not as cultivated as you.

JON
Please calm down.

JOAN
You calm down.

[Pause]

JON
Let me put it this way.

The US—our country—committed terrible wrongs against Native Americans, African black people, and, arguably, women.

JOAN
Why arguably?

JON
Okay. Not arguably.

The point I'm trying to establish is that these wrongs should be redressed. But to exact vengeance on all white heterosexual males irrespective of when they lived is not the best way—

JOAN

What is the best way?

Are the Native Americans better off now than they were after the Trail of Tears? Are black people really better off than they were during the hey-day of Jim Crow?

Black teens and adolescents are being shot to death every week.

And the white cops who murder them usually go free, right?

JON

Yes.

I aligned women with Native Americans and black people,

but the situation is not the same.

JOAN

Oh! So why did you "align" them?

[Pause]

JON

I can see this discussion is going nowhere.

Can't we just embrace and let it go?

Or at least put it on hold?

JOAN

Put it on hold until when?

If you're not giving any credence to my point of view what's the point of putting it on hold?

JON

I really don't know how to answer that, Joan.

JOAN

I'm leaving.

JON

Leaving?

Right now?

JOAN

Right now, yes.

JON

Why?

When will you be back?

JOAN

I don't know.

JON

This is crazy.

Don't leave.

Let's try to talk it over calmly.

JOAN

There is no more talking.

Not when you patronize and discredit me.

[Joan tries to get out of bed; Jon holds her shoulders]

JON

Don't go, Joan.

JOAN

You're hurting me!

Let go.

JON
[Releasing her]
Where are you going?

JOAN

None of your fucking business.

I'm going to a women's shelter.

I will show them the bruises on my shoulders.

I'll tell them what you did to me.

[Joan dresses quickly

Jon hears the door slam shut]

MANSON

PLAYERS

Charles Manson

Film Director

Guards

Cameraman

Charles Manson, 80 years old, is being filmed in a documentary called CHARLES MANSON SUPERSTAR.

The setting is a yard outside Pelican State Prison.

Manson is in arm and leg chains, but he can still shuffle.

There are four armed guards, two on each side.

The documentary director is to the left of the filming camera, a Black Magic URSA Mini Pro.

GUARD
Brought you your dentures.

MANSON
Good pig.

DIRECTOR
Pelican Bay has a rep as being hard-ass. How they treating you?

MANSON

Let me get my teeth right.

[Pause]

Repeat the question.

DIRECTOR

Pelican Bay has a rep as being hard-ass. How they treating you?

MANSON

How many hard-ass joints I been in my life?

Ain't nothing changed.

No, no, no, no.

Negativity, man.

If I ask for a bucket of shit they say: No fuckin' way, Manson.

DIRECTOR

Why are they so hard on you, do you think?

MANSON

They'd ruther see me dead is why.

 'Cept they fraid the fuckin' consequence.

There still folks out there love my skanky ass.

DIRECTOR

An early psychiatric analysis characterized you as "emotionally unstable, assaultive, dangerous, and bisexual."

You into boys or girls?

MANSON

What's your name again?

DIRECTOR

Pierre Grossman.

MANSON

You a Jew?

DIRECTOR

Does it matter?

MANSON

Yeah, it matters, motherfucker.

I ain't talkin to no Jew about my life and times.

Where did the "Pierre" come from?

DIRECTOR

My mother is French. I was born in France.

MANSON

That's different.

The French mostly understood my shit.

What you call this movie, Pierre?

DIRECTOR

It's a documentary.

I call it Charles Manson Superstar.

MANSON

Asshole title.

Another fucking cliché about Manson.

What's the question?

DIRECTOR

An early psychiatric analysis characterized you as "emotionally unstable, assaultive, dangerous, and bisexual." You into boys or girls?

MANSON

Whoa! Motherfucker.

You never heard?

Manson done had a fuckin' harem of beautiful chicklets.

DIRECTOR

Yet you fucked males in prison and you fucked them out of prison. It was reported that you held a straight razor to some dude's throat while you nailed him in the ass.

MANSON

Hard habit to break, Pierre.

You're a lightweight, I can see that.

If you was inside I'd have your ass and you'd love it.

DIRECTOR

Lot of folks think you emerged from some deep hole in Death Valley. But you had a mother, Kathleen Maddox.

MANSON

Das right.

Her people was Holy Rollers.

From Ashland, Kentucky.

She run away when she was fifteen.

Had me when she was sixteen. In Ohio.

My father's name was Kyle something, from Tennessee.

Never met the dude.

When Kathleen was sentenced to five years in Moundsville State Prison down there in Charleston, West Virginia, they sent me to Bennett.

DIRECTOR
What's that?

MANSON
Bennett Home for Boys. Clarksburgh, West Virginia.

I was ten years old.

DIRECTOR
Your mother was a prostitute?

MANSON
She didn't have no choice is how I see it.

DIRECTOR
What'd she get the five years for?

MANSON
Her brother Walter lived in West Virginia, which is where we moved from Ohio when I was not even a year old.

Walter didn't have no kind of real job and him and Kathleen they decided to rob a gas station in Charleston, West Virginia.

What they used was a full bottle of Dr. Pepper wrapped in a cloth bag which they tried to hit the attendant on the head with, but they messed up and got nabbed.

DIRECTOR

So what's the skinny on the Beatles' Helter Skelter?

MANSON

Ain't no skinny, Pierre.

Bunch of us on the ranch was stoned on acid and jivin' around.

It was some riot in a ghetto someplace, burn baby burn, and the White Album just come out which we was listening to.

So we started messin' 'round with the lyrics an shit.

That was it.

I never gave a shit about the Beatles.

DIRECTOR

Is it true that you had in mind to set up some kind of desert military force, after the example of Rommel who outfoxed the Brits in the North African campaign?

MANSON

I had all kinds of shit in mind one time or 'nother.

You drop acid a bunch your mind gets to zoomin'.

Mostly, I just wanted to be left alone with my coyotes and scorpions and my music.

DIRECTOR

There was a story that you were arrested while living in a den with two of your girls, protected by coyotes.

MANSON

I spent most my life in jail.

When I was outta jail I was a city dude.

Death Valley was the first time I come across desert.

But I felt right at home.

The coyotes and scorpions, they loved and protected me.

DIRECTOR
Desert god.

Yet you said at the trial:

"I ain't no god. I ain't nothing but a half-assed thief."

MANSON
Reckon.

Trial was a long damn time ago.

DIRECTOR
You recall, at the same trial, saying, "I am the god of fuck"?

MANSON
You're a Jew punk so you don't know that being a half-assed thief don't mean I don't know how to fuck.

I said the god of fuck deal to Squeaky Fromme first time I done her.

In my van.

Go ask her how she liked it.

DIRECTOR
Was it Squeaky Fromme that tasted Sharon Tate's blood off the knife and said: "Freaky shit, I like it"?

MANSON
That was Susan Atkins. Sadie.

Whatever Sadie said, you could be sure it was a lie.

DIRECTOR
Sadie turned on you, right?

MANSON
Became a born again.

That's what she claimed.

Bought her some sympathy, but didn't get her ass sprung.

Before she come to the ranch she was a devil worshiper with what's his face up there in San Francisco. LaVey.

Mindfuck was her deal.

Whatever Sadie did Sadie wanted to be top dog.

Fucking included.

With me that was never happening, you dig?

She claimed I was God.

Which is dog spelled backwards.

I never dug her, never trusted her.

She even smelled funky. Her skin, her hair.

DIRECTOR
Some folks like funky. Who smelled good?

MANSON
Linda Kasabian, Squeaky, Sandra Good, Leslie Van Houten, Mary Brunner. Ruth Ann Moorehouse smelled like star jasmine.

That was then.

Can't say how they smell now the law has got in their panties.

DIRECTOR

The sweet-smelling girls of the notorious Manson family.

Who was a better fuck—you or Tex Watson?

MANSON

Don't think I ever seen Tex not fucked up.

Way too stoned do more'n get his rocks off.

Myself? Took my time, knew just what the fem wanted.

And I done give it to her.

Just not all at once.

DIRECTOR

I heard that folks are still sending you gifts.

MANSON

Das right.

Just yesterday I got a black silk shirt.

Know what I done with it?

I twisted it into a voodoo doll and stuck pins in it.

Then I send it to one of the motherfuckers that talk shit 'bout me.

They let me send out my dolls at Pelican because they scared of me.

Know what happens next?

Human that received my doll dies a painful death.

I have your address, Pierre Grossman.

Expect a gift from Manson.

Gonna keep you from sleepin' at night.

[Pause]

DIRECTOR
Folks don't know this about you: You were married.

MANSON
[Shouting to the camera man]
You behind the camera!

Don't duck, bro.

I see your ass.

Look at me!

You're Irish, right?

What's your name?

CAMERAMAN
Timothy Leary.

MANSON
Right.

Good Irish name.

Bless you, Timothy Leary.
[To the director]
What did you say, Pierre?

DIRECTOR
You were married, right?

MANSON
Yup. Had me a taste of that shit.

Got married in 1955 to the first girl I fucked.

 I ain't lyin'.

I was 21 and all my sex had been in the joint.

Reform school, juvenile hall, state prison.

With dudes, okay?

So I got married in Indianapolis.

Had me a son.

Then I was arrested and sent to Terminal Island.

That's a federal penitentiary in San Pedro, California, because I was transporting stolen goods over state lines.

My wife hung in there long as she could.

DIRECTOR
What's her name?

MANSON
Won't say. Her or my son's name neither.

Let 'em live in peace.

When I get out we'll see.

DIRECTOR
They ever get in touch?

MANSON
Won't say nothin' more about it.

DIRECTOR
Thinking of getting out?

MANSON
Never can tell.

DIRECTOR

How long you been inside?

I'm 80 now. Been in 68 years altogether.

DIRECTOR

So your wife and son abandon you while you're serving time.

You get out of Terminal Island in 1967. What happens next?

MANSON

No. I get out after they transfer me from Terminal Fed to McNeil Island State Prison, up in Washington.

What happens next?

Find me some fems and turn 'em out.

DIRECTOR

You became a pimp.

MANSON

Ya mon.

You half French so you must know that deep down every broad wants to be a ho.

And I was real good at seeing they got what they wanted.

And it bought me time to set around, get stoned, do my music.
[Shouting at the guards]:
Yo, pig!

Get me some water.
[Both guards start]
[To the director]:
You see them pig-guards, Pierre?

One's black, the other's white.

They fight to see which of them will get on my good side.

I fucked both of them and now they love me and are scared of me.

DIRECTOR
Where and when was your first rape?

MANSON
Bennett, like I said before.

Bennett Home for Boys. Clarksburgh, West Virginia.

I was ten years old, the youngest, smallest kid in the joint.

Seven bigger kids--they gang-raped me.

When I got it together to go to the assistant superintendent, motherfucker called Fish, he told me pull my pants down, bend over and show him where they got me.

Then he spit tobacco juice on his hand and shoved it up my ass.

Then he said to the guard:

"Okay, he's primed, let them fuck his brains out."

I never got a chance to even things up with Fish, but that night at about three a.m. I took a window crank--one them steel rods about sixteen inches long, weighin' about three pounds--and went to the bunk of the first dude that fucked my ass.

I hit him eight or nine blows hard as I could hit to the head and face.

About killed him. Too fuckin' bad I dint.

[Pause]

DIRECTOR

Shorty Shea.

MANSON

Ranch hand on Spahn's Ranch.

Got into my business more'n once cuz he was jealous of all my beautiful fems.

He had a hardon for Linda Kasabian, but she just laughed at him.

Ended up getting hisself offed and cut up in small chunks.

But not by me.

DIRECTOR

You sure about that?

MANSON

Was never charged.

DIRECTOR

Father Flanagan's Boys Town.

MANSON

They sent my ass there after I busted out of Bennett.

But I bust out of Flanagan like four days after I got there, me and some other kids.

Stole cars, broke into stores an' shit.

Even held up one old guy and slapped him around a little bit.

They caught us five days later.

Sent me to Prideaux Juvenile Detention in Indiana, which was shitty.

But I wasn't 'bout to do no time at no Father Motherfucker's

Boy's Town.

DIRECTOR

Lotsapoppa.

MANSON

Three hundred pound black dude.

Bragged he was a Black Panther which he never was.

He tried to zap me because of a drug deal gone sour.

I zapped him first.

He had his paws 'round my neck when I shot one round in his belly with an old Buntline .22.

That's a small caliber pistol but he slid down dead like a sack of shit.

DIRECTOR

You have a problem with black folks.

MANSON

That's what they been saying all this time, but it ain't no truth to it. Like Danny DeCarlo, the Straight Satan biker that lived on the ranch, he hated blacks, and when he'd rap with me I'd like nod my head. So he'd go away sayin': Charlie agrees with me.

But I was just reflectin' back what he hisself thought.

Yo, I been in prison all my life, and that's the first thing you learn: go wit' the flow unless you big enough and shit-eating enough to bust some skulls.

DIRECTOR

What about those Latino gang members who set you on fire?

MANSON

I was a young dude, early on in Sing Sing.

Most folks dint know who I was.

Was in the yard.

Puerto Rican gang.

They poured gas on me and lit a match.

It dint amount to much.

There was five and five of them died the next year.

I won'r say how.

DIRECTOR

Did you know the name Sharon Tate before you murdered her?

MANSON

Wasn't me that murdered her, Pierre.

I didn't know her cuz I never seen none of her movies.

DIRECTOR

Whether you actually murdered or not, you're responsible for a whole lot of deaths. Sharon Tate, her unborn baby.

Coffee heiress Abigail Folger and her playboy lover.

The LaBiancas.

Hairdresser to the stars, Jay Sebring.

Gary Hinman. Young Steven Parent. Lotsapoppa.

Who knows who else?

Didn't you once say you murdered thirty-five humans?

MANSON

Thirty-five, sixty-five.

Who the fuck counts?

But what about you motherfuckers out there in freedomland?

You're murderers.

Tearing into that red meat with your teeth while watchin' fuckin' TV.

DIRECTOR

I forgot. You're a vegetarian.

How do you feel about all the innocent people you killled?

MANSON

Here's something for you to think about, Jew.

Being rich don't mean being innocent.

Myself? I feel great.

Don't I look like I'm feelin' great?

DIRECTOR

You look like Manson with the satanic glint and home-made swastika tat on your forehead.

You have a thing for Nazis?

MANSON

Nazis are cool.

Monsters like me.

DIRECTOR

Is that what you are?

MANSON

That's what you done made me.

The Monster!

You fear me and you want to fuck me.

DIRECTOR

Did you ever hear the name Roman Polanski?

MANSON

Polish ham.

DIRECTOR

That's a joke, right?

But you never even break a smile.

When was the last time you had an honest-to-God belly laugh?

MANSON

When I heard that plane go down over Scotland 'cause of some terrorist attack.

Bunch of people killed an' shit.

For some reason that got me in the funny bone.

DIRECTOR

You mean Lockerbie, Scotland. That was in the Eighties.

Long time to go without laughing.

MANSON

When I feel like laughing I fart.

DIRECTOR

Which reminds me. You still doing that jive music of yours?

MANSON

Now and then.

When I can fit it into my busy schedule.

Wanna hear some riffs?

DIRECTOR

Maybe later, after your execution.

MANSON

There wasn't no death sentence when they done sentenced me.

Remember them voodoo dolls I was talkin' 'bout?

I got one wit your French Jew name on it: Pierre Grossman.

You 'bout to die before you get your Manson movie done.

DIRECTOR

Some people have wondered about this:

How come you talk in different ways?

Sometimes you sound Appalachian, other times like a hippie.

Still other times you talk in black vernacular.

And then you'll pull a white middle class speech.

MANSON

I imitate the way fools talk.

Whole lotta fools out there.

I move quick one to 'nother.

Keep yawl off-balance.

DIRECTOR
Who's your favorite serial killer? Excluding yourself.

[MANSON turns his back without responding; motions to the guards to take him back inside]

BUD & NORMA JEANE

PLAYERS

Marlon "Bud" Brando

Marilyn Monroe (Norma Jeane)

Two speakers offstage

Bud and Norma Jeane lookalikes lie on a king-sized circular waterbed beneath a ceiling mirror. They remain in bed throughout the drama, and their scenes are enacted while they are in bed.

Otherwise the stage is empty.

Norma Jeane, naked, is stretched out on her stomach.

NORMA JEANE

Can you see my feet in the mirror?

BUD

Yes.

NORMA JEANE

Do you like my feet?

BUD

Yes.

NORMA JEANE
Do you like my ankles?

BUD
Yes.

NORMA JEANE
Do you like my knees?

BUD
Yes.

NORMA JEANE
Do you like my thighs?

BUD
I'm crazy about your thighs.

NORMA JEANE
Do you like my shoulders?

BUD
Yes.

NORMA JEANE
I think they are not slender enough. Do you like my arms?

BUD
Yes.

NORMA JEAN
Do you like my ass?

BUD

Yes, dear. It so happens that I adore your ass.

NORMA JEANE

Do you like my breasts?

BUD

Yes.

NORMA JEANE

Do you like my face? My lips, nose, eyes? My ears?

BUD

Yes, every millimeter of every feature.

NORMA JEANE

Then you love me totally.

BUD

Totally. Tenderly. Tragically.

SPEAKERS OFFSTAGE

SPEAKER 1

Brando and Monroe?

SPEAKER 2

Who else?

Circa 1953.

They referred to each other as Bud and Norma Jeane.

SPEAKER 1

Why?

SPEAKER 2

Love talk.

Bud was Brando's nickname, Norma Jeane was MM's real name.

SPEAKER 1

Which one is Bud and which one is Norma Jeane?

SPEAKER 2

Norma Jeane is the one who asks: "Do you like my ass?"

SPEAKER 1

Are you sure?

SPEAKER 2

No.

SPEAKER 1

So what did Bud and Norma Jeane do together besides fuck and admire each other's beauty.

Did they actually talk?

Did they frolic in the woods?

SPEAKER 2

They talked, yes.

After their fashion.

They laughed and played like children.

And—unusual for each of them—they didn't argue.

They went outside into public view.

But disguised.

Especially if they had to walk any distance.

Bud would wear drag—he'd be a nun, female police officer, Fortune-500 female exec.

Norma Jeane would wear a dark wig, nose putty, and baggy slacks and top to obscure her assets.

Sometimes she'd smoke a Cuban cigar.

SPEAKER 1
Where'd they go?

SPEAKER 2
Parks, playgrounds--

SPEAKER 1
Playgrounds!

What'd they do in playgrounds?

SPEAKER 2
I don't know what they did.

Watch the children?

Climb the monkey bars?

They were both agile at that time, remember.

They also frolicked--to use your word--in nature sanctuaries.

They liked birds.

Each carried high-end birding binoculars.

They had friendly competitions about who would see more species.

You know how competitive Brando is.

[Bud and Norma Jeane in Nature]

BUD
What'd you spot, NJ?

NORMA JEANE
An avocet and black-necked stilt.

BUD
No way, NJ.

Avocets and stilts need more water than in this fake Hollywood pond.

NORMA JEANE
Nope. Wrong, Bud.

They added avocets and stilts.

Also ducks and swans.

They're trying to make the ponds as realistic as possible.

BUD
Yeah. I believe it!

Fucking Hollywood ponds.

I hate that shit.

NORMA JEANE
What do you really have against Hollywood, Bud?

Don't lie to me.

BUD

Would I lie to you, my little pigeon?

I hate fucking Hollywood, and hate myself for being a part of it.

NORMA JEANE

What'd you spot, Bud?

BUD

A golden eagle at the very top of that fan palm.

People don't know this, but a golden has wider wings and is much fiercer than the bald eagle

NORMA JEANE

Where?

BUD

It took off.

You're lucky.

Golden eagles feast on beautiful, tempestuous females.

NORMA JEANE

I thought they feasted on moody, muscular males.

BUD

I feel horsey.

Let's go riding, NJ.

SPEAKER 1

They rode horses. Makes sense.

Did Norma Jeane ride side-saddle?

SPEAKER 2

No. But Bud did,

Brando in nun's garb riding side-saddle.

SPEAKER 1

In nun's garb without underwear.

SPEAKER 2

Hell, neither of them wore underwear.

SPEAKER 1

As in a Buñuel film.

SPEAKER 2

Buñuel—that's one director Brando and MM might have gotten along with. Buñuel worked with Dali, who was an even harder case than those two.

SPEAKER 1

You asked about Bud and Norma Jeane outside the bedroom.

They also went to museums and galleries.

Norma Jeane was crazy about the French Impressionists.

Bud was into Surrealism and Dada.

"Our Dada who art in Dada, Dada be thy name."

SPEAKER 2

Beckett?

SPEAKER 1

Hemingway.

With a few alterations.

SPEAKER 2

Did Papa Hem ever do Norma Jeane?

SPEAKER 1

Papa Hem was impotent.

He tried it with Marlene Dietrich and got exactly nowhere.

Same deal with Ingrid Bergman.

SPEAKER 2

I didn't know that.

SPEAKER 1

Brando met Hemingway once when he was filming *Viva Zapata*.

They didn't hit it off.

SPEAKER 2

Why am I not surprised?

[Bud and Norma Jeane in the Big Apple]

Bud is a nun and Norma Jeane is a schoolteacher with a grey wig and spectacles. The Metropolitan Museum is featuring an exhibit called Harlem on My Mind.

Harlem schoolchildren were invited to the exhibit, and when a little girl standing in line saw Bud in his nun's habit, she shouted: "There go Marlon Brando."

The other children laughed.

NORMA JEANE

Some nun!

That little girl saw right through you, Bud.

BUD

Black children are smart.

They gotta be to survive in this shitty world.

[Suddenly a paparazzo appears and, on one knee, is photographing Bud and Norma Jeane. Bud snatches his camera and exposes the film]

BUD

Get the fuck out of here.

PAPARAZZO

Is that any way for a nun to talk?

[Bud punches the paparazzo and bloodies his nose.

Then Bud and Norma Jeane commence their art-viewing]

[20 minutes later]

BUD

Did you enjoy that, NJ?

NORMA JEANE

Renoir always makes me hungry.

BUD

What do you feel like eating?

NORMA JEANE

Something with a lot of cream.

BUD

Let's go to the 4 Seasons.

We can change in the limo.

[Back in the bedroom]

SPEAKER 1

Okay. Now to the sex.

I'm guessing that it was savory?

SPEAKER 2

Maybe, maybe not.

The story is that Norma Jeane was not always an active participant.

She tended to be distracted.

Something like: *Welcome to the pleasure garden; pluck whatever you wish while I lie beneath you, Nembutal dreaming.*

SPEAKER 1

Ah, with Bud she was active and then some.

She wasn't doing a lot of drugs then.

Bud liked playing passive partner.

Norma Jeane really got into the domina role.

It was the reverse of how they were with other lovers.

Though not absolutely.

SPEAKER 2

Go on.

SPEAKER 1

Once Bud bound Norma Jeane with beautiful intricate knots.

He'd learned them in Japan while filming *Sayonara*.

When he finished tying her up, he said: "I'm going to lunch."

He returned 75 minutes later.

Usually, though, it was Norma Jeane doing Bud.

Sitting on his face while reading aloud from Dostoyevsky.

She read in the same voice she used to sing "Happy birthday, Mr. President" to JFK on his 45th birthday.

The celebration took place in Madison Square Garden, you recall.

Norma Jeane's sequined, flesh-colored gown was so tight she almost had to be sewn into it.

Sans underwear, of course.

Jackie K was not in attendance.

Three months later Norma Jeane is dead.

SPEAKER 2

Which Dostoyevsky did Norma Jeane read aloud while sitting on Bud's face?

SPEAKER 1

The Idiot.

SPEAKER 2

That's a big book.

SPEAKER 1

With Dostoyevsky you read and you scan.

Norma Jeane adored Prince Myshkin.

Epileptic, doomed, sainted.

SPEAKER 2

Bit melodramatic.

Though not unsexy in its way.

So Bud left Norma Jeane all trussed up and went out for lunch.

What did he have for lunch?

SPEAKER 1

With Bud you never knew.

It could be French fries and Mars bars.

He would come back with a villainous ketchup mustache.

It was a joke, they both laughed.

He undid her binds.

Or maybe they fucked first then he undid them.

SPEAKER 2

The SM role reversal and ketchup mustache are nice, but more or less commonplace in that Hollywood milieu, no?

Where in their sexual loving is the tenderness and the trage-dy that Bud pledged?

SPEAKER 1

It is everywhere, you fool.

SPEAKER 2

My question is: What did they locate in each other that was not available in all the other gorgeous movie stars with cosmetically enhanced attributes?

SPEAKER 1

Call this informed speculation.

They located their fundamental child in each other.

Bud found Quinn, his angel-twin who died at age 4.

Norma Jeane found a shadow version of her child-self: tormented, ambitious, self-hating, charismatic.

SPEAKER 2

"Fundamental child."

If I let you get away with that, who knows what you'll come up with next.

I know about Brando's feelings for the disadvantaged.

He worshipped humanity while mostly despising humans.

He felt himself a failed idealist.

What were Marilyn Monroe's ideals?

Could she even extend herself outside herself?

SPEAKER 1

The question is irrelevant.

As with Brando: The final measure of Marilyn Monroe must be her representation on celluloid.

Her two-dimensional radiance.

When a man took her loveliness in his arms, he took his life in his hands!

Her skin-tight red dress above the knees, steep décolletage, no underwear, her deliberate, dreamy, wiggling walk away from the mounted zoom.

Away from the panting worldwide audience.

Simulacrum of the forever vulnerable, unattainable golden-haired sex goddess, who, like Circe, transforms men into swine.

SPEAKER 2

If Norma Jeane is Circe, Bud must be Ulysses wending his way back to Ithaca.

SPEAKER 1

You know what you are?

A literalist of the imagination.

ARTAUD

I salute Antonin Artaud for his passionate, heroic negation of
everything that causes us to be dead while alive.

—André Breton

PLAYERS
ANTONIN ARTAUD (who is writing to JACQUES RIVIERE,
literary editor of the important journal *Nouvelle Revue Fran-*
***cais*)**

SETTING: Two desks opposite each other on an otherwise empty
stage. Riviere's desk, stage right, is large and ornate. Artaud's desk,
stage left, is small and weathered. Artaud, nervously, is at his desk,
but Riviere is absent.

Cher M. Jacques Riviere: **May 2, 1923**

You write that you, as literary editor of *Nouvelle Revue Francais*, will not

publish my submitted verses but that they nonetheless intrigue you and you

would be pleased to make my acquaintance if I would drop by your office

on Friday between 3:30 and 5:00 PM.

I reply in turn that that is very large of you, M. Jacques Riviere, very grand, *tres noblesse*, nobly pitying . . .

Or are you, like Zeus in his private capacity, predatory, looking for an easy thrill by diddling a confirmed madman?

If I were to inform you that my lunatic brain is now floating in Madame Andre Breton's bidet, a knuckle of turd black as uncolonized Africa, would you still be wishing to make my acquaintance, M. Jacques Riviere, literary editor of *Nouvelle Revue Francais?*

The facts are these: I presented you with my tormented heart, brain and viscera and you replied with literary exegesis. But now, privately, you would like to prick my diseased brain.

Goodbye,

Antonin Artaud

Cher M. Riviere: **May 12, 1923**

Your courteous letter is in hand. My left hand, which is where I make a point of holding all courteous letters from mainstream journal editors who reject my verses. You insist, with courtesy, that your regard for me does not resemble Zeus in his private capacity, but is actually a "humanistic" interest in my "manner of thinking."

May I inform you, *Monsieur*, that I detest the word "humanistic," and if that filthy adjective constitutes your interest in Antonin Artaud's "manner of thinking," you will be sorely disappointed and might as well grant the celebrated Andre Breton yet another interview. (He is always prepared to do interviews so long as he has his enormous sable *Kopf* photographed while doing all the talking).

If you, *cher maitre*, can find nothing suitably humanistic in my lugubrious verses, you will surely find my material person less humanistic still. First of all I have a mouth of foully rotting teeth. Moreover I am unwiped and unwashed (I detest the approach to my asshole and equally detest water); my stink will adhere to your office walls long after I take my leave.

Above all I am in constant, unrelieved torment; I am in fact a clinically diagnosed lunatic. Worse still, I have felt compelled to cultivate my lunacy, to structure and refine it. At my best—what you would call best—my bloodshot eyes dart every which way, I cough from deep in my malignant lungs and will be compelled to deposit rich pearly phlegm on your lacquered hardwood floor. Moreover, I fart repeatedly—that is, emit small shits. It is merely delirium. But do not fret, *Monsieur, Je ne suis pas dangereux.* Except to my diseased self and to the diseased world which I (and you, if only you recognized it) inhabit.

Monsieur, Recevez l'assurance de mes sentiment distingués,

Antonin Artaud

Cher Maitre: **June 12, 1923**

In your post of May 23 you attempt to explain your interest in my person vis-à-vis your decisive lack of interest in my verses. You write that it is the "extraordinary lucidity of [my] self-diagnosis" in contrast to the "general vagueness" of my verses which "fascinates" you. You go even farther with your impertinent suggestion that I attempt to apply that same lucidity to the verses themselves. Your point is that "intellectual force," such as I (according to you) present in my "self-diagnosis," demands a context which poetry would provide, rather than "aimlessly bleeding out into the absolute."

But what if I were to inform you that poetry and the so-called literary world, such as you have devoted your professional life to, mean to me nothing. Less than nothing. It is precisely the "bleeding out into the absolute" which alone compels me.

All I ask is that you attempt to palpate my brain, that blackened knuckle of turd floating in Madame Andre Breton's bidet. All I ask is that you respond to me with your bowels and balls and arteries which trail thickly from that switched-off organ in your chest. That is, *Monsieur*, the only way to respond to my verses. I know of course that you lack that capacity, indentured as you are to the normal, the "context," the anti-absolute, unless mediated by your holy ghost.

What if I were to inform you that your Jesus is counterfeit, a superimposition, that your false and bleeding Son of the Father is in fact the son of demonic Abaddon, my God.

Goodbye,

Antonin Artaud

M. Jacques Riviere   **July 8, 1923**

I am flattered by the offer you extended in your previous post of printing our correspondence in your esteemed journal, with some revision and with the fictionalizing of our names.

But why revise and fictionalize? Contrary to the usual versifiers who publish their poems or "memoirs" in the *Nouvelle Revue Francais,* my writings, imperfect as they may be, are who and what I am. I categorically refuse to fictionalize and "normalize" any utterance I make with my pen, my rotting mouth, my inflamed brain, or my holy unwiped asshole.

My agony is irreducible, *Monsieur*. My agony is infinitely modulated. My agony radiates like ten thousand suns to those who feel or sense. Why then must I edit and fictionalize?

 Van Gogh attempted suicide by shooting himself in the gut. But he didn't die, and in fact commenced to paint his strongest, most lunatic paintings as he was dying from the bullet in his belly. Crows over a wheat field contains what you would call imperfections but every brushstroke is filled with furious, pitying blood. If you were to rip apart Vincent's wheat it would erupt into fire, shit, sperm and phlegm, and bleed down on your exegetic head. That is how I view my own work, *Monsieur*, the dialectic between the canker in my gut and my ordered/disordered lines on the page.

In a word, I would be pleased and flattered to have our correspondence published in your esteemed arts and cultural journal, but only exactly as it stands, without falsification.

Je vous remercie, cher Maitre,

Antonin Artaud

Dear Sir: **October 9. 1923**

You apologize for not responding to my July 8 post, you withdraw your offer of publishing our correspondence, you withdraw your invitation to visit you in your office on Friday between 3:30 and 5:00 PM, and you inquire (tactfully) about my "suicidal ideation," presumably because of your humanistic concern for my welfare.

If I were to commit suicide my supreme despair would no longer radiate like twenty thousand suns.

If I were to commit suicide it would not be to atomize but to put myself in orbit around this filthied-over globe.
If I were to commit suicide I would no longer remain undead as the sole exemplar of your bottomless black hole.

If I were to commit suicide I would not inject morphine into my left thigh and dream of vomiting an impossible earth.

Not suicide, *Monsieur*, but not-to-have-been-born is my earnest, enfeebled wish. You would have to unchain that bloody organ in your chest to comprehend this.

Nonetheless, I appreciate your Christian concern for my soul. (Did you know that Breton goes to mass twice a week? You can recognize him in his pew by the amplitude of his sable head).

Here then I sing to you. It is in verse, *cher maitre*. Listen with your traitorous ear.

o dedi

a dada orzoura

o dou zoura

a dada skizi

Antonin Artaud

BATAILLE

PLAYERS

Georges Bataille

"God"

Speaker

Setting is a small "dungeon"-brothel on rue St-Denis, in the 2nd arrondissement, Paris. The Speaker is offstage.

GOD
[Sniggering]

Down on your knees.

These are my hairy parts.

Admire.

Merde, Don't touch . . .

Now touch.

Your tongue . . .thrust.

 Lick.

SPEAKER

Tatty little brothel on rue Saint-Denis.

Bataille is there weekly.

He swallowed a third of a gram of cocaine.

He is on his knees.

His wrists bound behind the back with one of her scented scarves.

[B couldn't identify the scent; his sinuses were congested]

GOD
Enough.

Lick there now.

My asshole.

Here, I spread it.

We call it *le petit* . . .

I can see you like that.

My name is God.

BATAILLE
I know very well that your name is God.

It is the name with which I christened you.

SPEAKER
For almost a year B had been visiting God weekly in her brothel dungeon.

Which was a sacrifice.

If he wanted to go more often, why didn't he?

It couldn't be money.

B was profligate with what little he had.

"Reckless expenditure" was a cardinal rule, allied to gift-giving, Potlatch.

It couldn't be the heavy doses of cocaine which pained his heart.

He welcomed the idea of dying squalidly in the throes.

BATAILLE
[Punctilious]
Why *le petit*, not *la petite?*

GOD
You know why.

BATAILLE
I don't.

Tell me.

GOD
Shut your cunty mouth.

 Lick.

SPEAKER
Variations of this exchange God improvised every visit.
From where B, wrists bound behind his back, knelt stiffly
at "le petit" de Dieu in the brothel dungeon on rue Saint-Denis,
he could, through the small filthied-over window above him,
see the fabled Centre Pompidou.

(Which in fact was not yet constructed; but fact is not a factor here)

The once-controversial, now weirdly comfortable architecture,
was constructed by Renzo Piano and Richard Rogers in 1977.
Neither of whom was French. So much for all-inclusive
French chauvinism ascribed to Gaul by its detractors.

GOD
How does it taste?

BATAILLE
[Gathering himself]
What?

GOD
How does it taste?

My hairy parts.

"Le petit?"

BATAILLE
[Erupting]
Like a baboon.

Like the knobby, shit-smeared hole of a baboon.

[GOD Laughs harshly, the gold tooth in the center of her mouth glitters]

SPEAKER
God wears black kid leather gauntlets extending up her slender arms. Her thick straw-colored hair is long enough for her to sit on.

Instead she gathers it in a loose bun at the top of her head, exposing her long neck and delicate ears.

A lavender rose is threaded through her hair. Like other Parisian prostitutes, she models herself on Toulouse-Lautrec's iconic Moulin Rouge can-can dancer
La Goulue.

She—God—is as supple as *La Goulue*, with her shapely legs in black stockings and the red heart embroidered on the seat of her knickers.

Bataille, groveling on the stone floor, isn't the least bit supple but he is intensely game.

Outside it is pouring rain.

God in her mauve peignoir, flourishing yellow hair piled high, face powdered ivory like a Geisha, lit cigarette in her carmine lips, is spread-eagled on a red divan, elevated. Her pertinent orifices are exposed and moist.

Bataille has removed his jacket and shoes but not his shirt, necktie, trousers, or black silk socks and garters.

With his stiff back, bound wrists, trick knee, garters and tuberculosis, groveling on the moldy dungeon floor beneath God, he is the very synecdoche of abjection.

BATAILLE
[Enraged. One miserable, bloodshot eye fastened on the Centre Pompidou which he could make out through the rain in the near distance through the squalid little window]

All the art that's fit to eat.

Rend, savage, lacerate, pulverize, obliterate.

SPEAKER
Stiff-shouldered, sex-mad, phthisic librarian.

B worked fifteen hours a week in the Bibliothèque Nationale.

Not sex-mad, sex-in-the-head-mad.

Death-mad *n'est-ce-pas*.

B boasted of having masturbated beside his mother's corpse.

He grew orgasmic just contemplating the infamous 1905

photo of the young opiated Chinese being mutilated in the so-called torture of the hundred pieces.

BATAILLE

The young and seductive Chinese man reduced to the work of the executioner, I adored.

He communicates his incommunicable pain to me, which is precisely what I was seeking, not to take pleasure in it, but to ruin in me that which is opposed to ruin.

Dehumanize me.

"Humanity" being insupportable.

Crown me by dehumanizing me.

Isolate the most obscenely erotic desire from conventional pleasure.

SPEAKER

"Sovereign" was one of B's crucial emblems.

Like his tormented, dehumanized, sovereign models Artaud and Lautréamont, Van Gogh and Sade.

BATAILLE
[To God]
Call me "Sade."

GOD

I call you Filth, Merde.

SPEAKER

Which is fine with B, the excremental vision being yet an-other principle of his life and work.

Like Luther of the Reformation, B was impacted, impossibly

constipated, hence his perhaps excessive valuation of joyous evacuation, reckless expenditure.

Why then did he restrict himself to divine punishment before God just once a week?

Because reckless expenditure represented his Sadean side.

Inhabiting the sovereign Marquis daily was a sweet punishment he must deny himself.

Remnant Roman Catholic in him.

B's Cartesian side.

Through the *merde* and incessant rain B could just see the Centre Pompidou, grown more popular with contemporary museum-goers than the somber, palatial Louvre.

The Centre Pompidou featured this month the dolls of Bellmer, the drawings of Masson, the just-discovered Henry Darger, and Pierre Klossowski (brother of Balthus, biographer of Sade).

Mad all, with the possible exception of Masson.

Featured also was the extreme makeover of Orlan, utterly mad.

As well as the paintings of the Surrealist autocrat Andre Breton.

Tireless (un-mad) advocate of the idealized dream.

B's lifetime enemy.

B detested idealism and equally detested those who thought otherwise.

Breton with his shock of sable hair and broad forehead never missed a photo-op.

There was no end to photos of the Surrealists taken en-masse, with Breton's massive head always featured.

Moreover, Breton was a moralist, a closet-Christian.

Which B professed to detest most of all.

When B's mistress, whom he abused, died of consumption and her mother wished to have a priest administer last rites, B erupted.

He would, he said, throttle any priest who dared enter his house.

This from the pale male who'd earlier converted to Roman Catholicism, spent a year as a Benedictine novice and cherished self-denial no less than reckless expenditure.

Except on the occasions he ingested opium and thus briefly loved his enemies, B's hate lacerated him, kept him thrashing in his bed at night.

Why then didn't he ingest opium more frequently?

Fearful of addiction?

No. Loving his enemies discomfited him.

Moreover, opium depressed his crucial sex-in-the-head urge.

Beneath the invariable suit and tie.

Beneath the pale, stiff, placid exterior which epitomized the French haut bourgeois, resided Bataille the abject.

Debauched, unregenerate hater, *battler*.

On behalf of his sacred knobby, shit-smeared hole.

On behalf of what Sartre (another long-time enemy) called *Le Néant*.

B, infinitely wrathful in his hairshirt and necktie,
stubbornly, recklessly charting his phenomenology of no thing.

GOD

I will piss you.

Open your mouth, Merde.

SPEAKER

God, pissing, sings through her lit cigarette (Gitanes, *sans
filtre*), one supple, black-stockinged leg askance.

GOD

Swallow God's gift.

SHREDDED WHEAT

PLAYERS

Brand

Actor

Audience

Stage is empty

ACTOR

Why are some humans called brands, Brand?

BRAND

Humans are called brands because they market and whore themselves.

ACTOR

Why are some humans called actors?

BRAND

International bad humans are called actors because they play the roles laid out for them.

ACTOR

Who uses the terms actor and brand?

BRAND

Fools and mofos who themselves are brands and actors use the terms actors and brands.

ACTOR

I hear it on TV a lot.

[Pause]

BRAND

Well what do you want to do, Actor?

ACTOR

Um. Can you read me more Samuel Beckett?

AUDIENCE

Borrring!

[Loud groans]

BRAND

Beckett in the AM!

It's a lovely morning.

Look at that chartreuse sky.

Smell that spicy smog.

Listen to those police sirens.

To protect and serve.

They're after another black actor, Actor.

ACTOR

Who?

BRAND

The police.

He's 16, black, long legs, wearing a hoodie & purple & green Nikes.

ACTOR

You said actors were international.

BRAND

Except for black folks.

They're actors wherever they are.

Let's go out, don't forget your mask.

ACTOR

Let's go to the park.

BRAND

What park?

ACTOR

Between Pfizer and Goog.

BRAND

That's a biosphere, not a park.

Erected by corporate mofos.

What do you want to do there, Actor?

ACTOR

Toss the frisbee.

BRAND

Where is the frisbee?

ACTOR

Under my pillow.

BRAND

Well go fetch it.

[Pause]

ACTOR

It's not there, Brand.

BRAND

The frisbee is not under your pillow?

ACTOR

No.

BRAND

Where is it then?

ACTOR

In the closet.

BRAND

Look in the closet, Actor.

ACTOR

It's not in the closet, Brand.

AUDIENCE

Check your asshole, Asshole!

[Derisive hoots]

BRAND

Did you look under your bed?

ACTOR

No.

[Pause]

It was under my bed, Brand.

BRAND

Okay.

ACTOR

It has a hole in it.

BRAND

The frisbee has a hole in it?

How did that happen?

ACTOR

That nasty cop patrolling the park stuck his penknife in it.

Then he twisted the hole to make it wider.

BRAND

I don't remember that.

ACTOR

I was tossing the frisbee with ZED.

You were at the chiropractor.

BRAND

We can play chess if we find an available table.

If there's no table we can play in the grass.

ACTOR

I have hay fever, remember?

BRAND

I said grass but it's astroturf or another artificial surface.

Get the chess set, Actor.

ACTOR

The queen is missing.

BRAND

We can use a small stone for the queen.

AUDIENCE

Use a small turd for the queen!

[Loud guffaws]

ACTOR

Both knights are missing.

And a rook.

BRAND

When did all those pieces go missing?

ACTOR

When I was playing chess with ZED last week.

You were at the dentist.

AUDIENCE
Fuck chess!

Where are the beach bunnies?

[Hoots, laughter]

ACTOR
We can ride our bikes, Brand.

BRAND
We only have one bike.

And it has a flat.

ACTOR
Didn't we repair the flat?

BRAND
We still have just one bike.

ACTOR
We can take turns.

BRAND
Bad idea, Actor.

ACTOR
What time is it?

BRAND
10:47.

ACTOR
I'm hungry.

BRAND

You ate breakfast, I saw you.

ACTOR

I ate what was left of the shredded wheat.

There wasn't much left.

I have an idea, Brand.

BRAND

What's that?

ACTOR

Let's go grocery shopping.

BRAND

Bad idea.

Grocery shopping is the shits, you know that.

[Pause]

ACTOR

What's left?

BRAND

Murder is left.

Let's murder a bad actor, Actor.

AUDIENCE

Yeah! Yeah!

[Raucous laughter]

ACTOR

I thought bad actors were international.

Except for black folks.

BRAND

We live in LA, remember?

International bad actors are all over the turf.

ACTOR

Like who, Brand?

BRAND

Wide choice.

Jews, Muslims, Chinatown, Japantown, Koreatown . . .

ACTOR

You're a Jew, Brand.

BRAND

Not so loud.

I'm only part Jewish.

A very small part.

ACTOR

Sounds like Jewish self-hatred, Brand

BRAND

Not so loud.

I only hate myself a little, Actor.

[Pause]

ACTOR

Weren't the Koreans responsible for Covid?

BRAND

You're thinking of the Chinese.

ACTOR

Right.

I meant the Chinese.

BRAND

So you want to murder us some Chinese?

ACTOR

Sure.

Murder Chinese or buy more shredded wheat at the grocery.

BRAND

Well, which do you prefer?

ACTOR

Can I think about it?

AUDIENCE

Murder the fuckin' Chinks, assholes!

[Hoots. raucous laughter]

BRAND

Well?

ACTOR

I'd rather buy shredded wheat at the grocery store, Brand?

BRAND

I knew you'd say that.

Don't forget your mask.

[At the grocery store]

ACTOR

They're out of shredded wheat, Brand.

BRAND

Buy Cheerios.

ACTOR

I don't like Cheerios.

BRAND

Buy Raison Bran.

ACTOR

They're out of Raison Bran

BRAND

Buy Grape Nuts.

I see them on the second shelf, to the left.

ACTOR

Okay.

We have bananas in the house, right?

BRAND
Probably.

ACTOR
Um. I forgot to take my wallet, Brand.

BRAND
You forget your wallet on a regular basis, Actor.

ACTOR
Sorry.

AUDIENCE
Borrring!

Get on with it, assholes!

BRAND
Well, that's done.

What now?

ACTOR
I'm going to eat some Grape Nuts with a sliced banana.

Want to join me, Brand?

BRAND
No, I don't.

[Later]

BRAND
Are you ready, Actor?

ACTOR

For what, Brand?

BRAND

Murder us some Chinese, remember?

AUDIENCE

Off the friggin Chinks already!

[Loud guffaws]

ACTOR

I'm ready, Brand.

Where to?

How about the Chinese laundry?

BRAND

That could work.

ACTOR

The guy I go to is small and skinny.

Real old.

I think he's real old, it's hard to tell,

He's only a block and a half away.

How do we murder him?

BRAND

That's the question.

A gun is noisy, a knife is messy.

ACTOR

We don't have a gun.

The only knives we have are kitchen knives.

BRAND

True.

ACTOR

We can pick him up and throw him down, Brand.

BRAND

Well, let's have a look at him.

Chinese are tricky.

A lot of them know martial arts.

[At the Chinese laundry]

BRAND

It says closed until after Memorial Day, Actor.

ACTOR

Yeah.

I forgot to mention that.

AUDIENCE

Fuck that shit! Assholes!

[Derisive hoots]

ACTOR

I'm tired, Brand.

Can we go back home?

BRAND

You're tired?

We haven't done anything except grocery shop for Grape Nuts.

ACTOR

I know.

Maybe I've caught Covid.

BRAND

I don't think so.

What do you want to do when we get home, Actor?

ACTOR

Read me some more Samuel Beckett.

BRAND

I've read you Yeats and Keats and Emily Dickinson.

What is it about Beckett that so intrigues you?

ACTOR

I don't know.

AUDIENCE

Not that again!

Fuck you two assholes!

Fuck Samuel Beckett!

[Boos, hisses]

SALAAM

PLAYERS

Elderly Israeli shop owner

Shop owner's daughter

Palestinian teenager

Palestinian's sister

Door to a small grocery store in Jerusalem, center stage.

Young Palestinian enters.

The Palestinian is slender, with black eyes and the tracings of a black mustache.

The Israeli shop owner is wiry with bloodshot eyes and a once black now grey and white mustache.

They glare into each other's eyes.

When the Palestinian opens his shirt displaying the explosives taped to his chest the Israeli shop owner on the crowded Jerusalem street points to the large pot simmering on the stove.

It contains cabbage, potatoes, green onions, and--unmistakably--a tiny human hand.

PALESTINIAN

I know that hand. It is my sister's hand.

ISRAELI

You are wrong.

It is my sister's hand.

PALESTINIAN

The hand is tiny.

You are an old man.

ISRAELI

I was young then as you.

In another country.

[Pause]

So you are a suicide bomber.

PALESTINIAN

Freedom fighter.

ISRAELI

Murdering hundreds of anonymous Jews will provide this freedom?

PALESTINIAN

You have left us no other way.

ISRAELI

You have heard of the word genocide?

PALESTINIAN

Every day of my life I hear this word.

ISRAELI

What is it that you want?

PALESTINIAN

The Jews to give us back our land.

That we can live in peace.

ISRAELI

And if I tell you this land in Jerusalem and beyond is not yours but ours? Historically ours?

PALESTINIAN

Let the United Nations decide.

ISRAELI

And the Jew-haters in the United Nations?

What about them?

PALESTINIAN

If you Jews are hated it is with reason.

ISRAELI

We are long familiar with being hated.

PALESTINIAN

Because we Muslims have had to defend ourselves, we too are lied about and hated.

[Pause]

ISRAELI

You will not win a war with Israel.

Despite that, you "freedom fighters" are prepared to murder yourself and hundreds of ordinary people you do not know who happen to be Jews.

Why?

Because of a principle?

PALESTINIAN

If this principle means truth, then yes, God willing, I am prepared to join my martyred freedom-fighting brothers and sisters.

ISRAELI

There are many others who feel as you do?

PALESTINIAN

I cannot give numbers.

But I have never met a Palestinian who was not prepared to die for freedom.

ISRAELI

And if you did meet one?

PALESTINIAN

I would refuse to shake his hand.

ISRAELI

Didn't Jordan abandon the Palestinians?

And why does the Arab League not support you?

Yet your rage is directed solely against Israel.

Why?

PALESTINIAN

Arabs are brothers.

Nobody has murdered our women and children but Israel.

Nobody has bulldozed our homes after a child throws a stone at your tanks but Israel.

ISRAELI

Israel has never struck the Palestinians without cause.

PALESTINIAN

That is a lie.

You Jews are cannibals.

ISRAELI

The opposite is true.

We have been cannibalized.

PALESTINIAN

You are talking about Nazis.

You cannot stop talking about your Nazis.

ISRAELI

No.

PALESTINIAN

That is the problem with you Jews.

You live in the past.

ISRAELI

No. We live in the present under the weight of the past.

There is no other way.

PALESTINIAN

These Nazis that so obsess you.

You have become them.

ISRAELI

What are you saying?

PALESTINIAN

Just that.

You Israelis in your crisp uniforms with your advanced weapons

slaughter us and degrade us as the Nazis did you.

ISRAELI

What you are parroting here I have heard before.

It has become fashionable.

It is an unspeakable slander.

And coming from you, a jihadi, with genocide taped and strapped across your body!

Then, as the young Palestinian raises his fist, the old Jew raises his arm with numbers tattooed on it.

The young man pronounces the word Palestine even as the old man utters the word Auschwitz.

Each in his own tongue.

[Blackness. When the lights come on the scene, still in the small shop, has shifted to the Palestinian's sister and the Israeli shop owner's daughter]

The Palestinian freedom fighter enters the shop and opens her blouse to display the explosives taped to her body.

In response, the Israeli shop owner's daughter gestures to her own breast.

They gaze long into each other's dark eyes.

[Pause]

The Palestinian jerks her head to the side, reaches under her blouse, detonates.

[That is one version. The other version follows]

After looking long at each other, the Palestinian freedom fighter nods her head once, slowly.

Carefully, she disarms the explosives.

Then she and the shop owner's daughter embrace and arm in arm step out into the turbulent Jerusalem street.

JIMI/JANIS/JM

PLAYERS

Jimi Hendrix
Speaker

SETTING is an empty stage with counterculture-style posters and paraphernalia on the walls. An expressive actor center-stage impersonates Jimi Hendrix at his custom guitar with recorded Jimi Hendrix riffs chimed in. Between riffs and occasional Jimi musings, Jimi fusses with his guitar while a "speaker" offstage recites his "story."

SPEAKER

September 18, 1970, Jimi Hendrix is found dead in the Samarkand Hotel in London. He spent the night with a German girlfriend and died in bed reportedly after drinking wine, doing meth, swallowing nine Vesparax sleeping pills, then asphyxiating on his own vomit. 27-years-old.

JIMI

Shit, can't be morning

Crawl naked, unsteady out of waterbed, nameless hotel, anywhere city

Ceiling mirror shattered & stained from group-grope the night before or night before that

Spike good-morning OJ with liquid meth slip on tasseled

leathery something smelling of smoke & patchouli

Run my fingers through my hair

Zombie out to the elevator, press **P** for penthouse

Ah, my cats are at the bar, but who the fuck are they?

Man, it's them honky writers from Rolling Stone & Craw-daddy

Fucking 8:20 in the morning

Get pissed on Irish coffee while juking the honkies

Back in my suite phone rings don't pick up

Smoke a joint have a bath

Drop three Percs

Rap on the phone to someone

Sip brew while rehearsing for tonight's gig

Drop acid—300 mcgs of Sunshine--do the gig

Mess with groupies smoke hash cut with meth eat half a tuna sandwich vomit drop four Seconals shattered collapse into sleep

SPEAKER

From the start Jimi always seemed to long for the next best thing to being dead. He didn't like to go out and preferred smack and barbiturates to booze.

He'd pull the curtains, turn the lights down, get stoned, and sit on his bed tuning his guitar.

He suffered from depressed panic attacks.

Could be he had undiagnosed autism or Asperger's Syndrome. At the same time he needed to be center-stage, numero uno.

The more famous he became the harder it became it play alongside him.

No matter what was rehearsed, Jimi would solo, playing what he wanted, how he wanted, taking as long as he wanted.

He'd play the guitar behind his back, with his teeth, his tongue. He'd set his guitar on fire.

Some gigs he'd keep his back to the audience and just tune his guitar.

Or he'd stop in the middle of a riff and mumble something to the audience:

JIMI

Planet earth to the sun: I ain't your fuckin' flunky no more.

SPEAKER

Jimi's music was not precisely rock, jazz, soul or blues, but could slide in and out of every one of those modes, even in a single session.

Jimi's severe depression and downer intake didn't affect his potency.

For a period of two or three years another paternity suit seemed to surface every few weeks.

He was a fave with groupies who cast rock stars' erect cocks in plaster. He slashed his wrists twice or three times but didn't die.

He was Black, Cherokee and Mexican but had no politics.

Somehow the racial anger visible everywhere at that time washed over him. JimI wore his hair fuzzy but it wasn't a 'fro.

JIMI

My hair is electric, man. It picks up all the vibes.

SPEAKER

He didn't like to talk, and when interviewed tended to play the genius from another planet. A survey by Rolling Stone in 2003 selected Jimi Hendrix as the greatest guitarist in rock history.

* * *

PLAYERS

Janis Joplin

Speaker

SETTING is an empty stage with counterculture-like posters and paraphernalia, An actor center-stage impersonates Janis Joplin (Pearl) belting out the blues; recorded Janis Joplin blues are chimed in. Between riffs and Janis musings, a "speaker" offstage recites her "story."

SPEAKER

October 4, 1970: Janis Joplin is found dead in her room at the Landmark Hotel in Hollywood, California. Alcohol, Percodan and heroin are found in her system. The official cause is accidental heroin overdose. 27-years-old.

[Traveling from Port Arthur, Texas to the West Coast for the first time]

JANIS

I want to smoke dope, take dope, lick dope, suck dope, fuck dope.

SPEAKER

It is documented that she fulfilled every one of those resolutions before she OD'd in LA at age 27.

She hated listening to "whitebread" rock so it was a revelation when she heard recordings of Bessie Smith, then Leadbelly.

(These were the anti-racist 60s, otherwise Janis might have modeled her "blues" on Ethel Merman).

Janis recalled her mama telling her as a young girl: "Janis, think before you speak."

But she couldn't hold back didn't want to hold back. Except for stone blues nobody was singing their pain.

Black militants like Stokely Carmichael and the Panthers dissed the blues for "celebrating black victimization."

Janis didn't hear blues that way.

Her politics could probably be summed up in her repeated lament: "Why can't people just learn to dig each other?"

She wore feathers, beads, bells and patchouli, which looked weird in the daytime, but cool onstage when she strutted her shit and everyone was stoned. She had a small tattoo of a bleeding heart on her left breast.

In the last year of her life she was in the process of metamorphosing into "Pearl," an even rawer image, more hooker than hippie.

Blues are typically about backdooring or being backdoored;

fretting over love or causing someone to fret over your love.

Janis's blues were about fretting over unrequited love.
She belted it better than she lived it.

She came on so heavy with cats she wanted to get it on with,
she'd drive them away.

Or if someone balled her, the mo'fucker would do it once
then split.

On the other hand, if a dude came on like a groupie, she
wouldn't dig it:

JANIS

I don't want no ass-kisser.

I want a cat that's bigger, ballsier than me.

But when I'm pullin' my shit the only cats that hang around
dressing rooms are flunkies.

Ain't no man in the world needs to hang around a dressing
room.

SPEAKER

She identified with Zelda Fitzgerald: mad, maddening, ad-
dicted to a child's innocence, only with the big voice, tits,
patchouli, Southern Comfort, primo dope, and a fuck-ready
stud in the wings.

While on the road, she read but never finished reading *Look
Homeward Angel*, which details in a thousand pages or so
the impossibility of going back.

BB King, always generous, said: "Janis Joplin sings the
blues as hard as any black person."

Janis did everything hard, hot, loud, brassy. Then she'd
break just like a little girl.

* * *

PLAYERS

JIM MORRISON

SPEAKER

SETTING is an empty stage with posters of Rimbaud, Artaud, and Native American paraphernalia. An actor center-stage impersonates Jim Morrison in leather pants, crooning, with recorded Morrison music chimed in. Between riffs and occasional JM musings, a "speaker" offstage recites JM's "story."

SPEAKER

July 3, 1971. Jim Morrison, like the French revolutionary Marat, was found in the bathtub in his Paris apartment at 17 Rue Beautreillis, by his girlfriend, Pamela Courson. According to the "official" report, the cause of death was heart failure aggravated by heavy drinking. Because no autopsy was conducted, rumors that Morrison died of a heroin or cocaine overdose made the rounds. A small plaque marks his burial site in the Père Lachaise Cemetery in Paris. 27-years-old.

SPEAKER

Toward the end of their tortured love affair, fueled by hashish and absinthe, the poet Rimbaud watched from the window as the older poet Verlaine carried a dead fish in one hand and a bottle of olive oil in the other to prepare dinner.

RIMBAUD
[Laughing, shouts from the window]
You look ridiculous!

SPEAKER

When Verlaine, enraged, gets upstairs, he slaps Rimbaud across the face with the dead fish. Then he leaves, slamming the door.

This happened in the Soho district of London.

The next time they met, about a week later in Brussels, a drunken Verlaine pulled out a small caliber pistol and fired two shots at Rimbaud, who was wounded in the elbow, and fled.

Rimbaud, age 19 or thereabouts, stops writing poetry, joins the Dutch army, deserts in Java, moves to Cyprus, finally settles on the Horn of Africa, where, reportedly, he becomes a gun runner then a slave trader.

Slave trading would seem to contradict Rimbaud's earlier support of the Paris Commune.

Contradictions were of course Rimbaud's MO. The Doors' leading devil admired Rimbaud.

Like Rimbaud, JM disordered his senses to write and perform.

One night in 1968 Morrison and Janis Joplin got filthy drunk at a Hollywood party and had their arms draped over each other's shoulders.

But then JM turned mean and grabbed Janis by the hair, pulling her head into his crotch, holding it there.

Finally she broke free, fleeing into the bathroom in tears. JM was wrestled into a car.

Janis ran after him, reached inside the car and hit JM on the head with a bottle of Southern Comfort.

JM was rubbing his head and laughing as the car pulled away.

Both rock supernovas were in character:

The American Rimbaud, drunk, capriciously cruel.

The intensely bereft white blues-belter from Port Arthur, Texas, who would trade it all to be beautiful and land her man.

To the media, Morrison claimed to be committed to revolt, anarchy, and chaos. He was bullshitting, spouting counter-culture doctrine.

Homeless people disgusted him and so did welfare recipients. He was known to use the N-word when referring to black people.

Though he disowned his family, the privileged milieu in which he was raised was hard to kick.

Like Rimbaud, who stopped writing and doping at age 19, Morrison several times talked about faking his death and "splitting to Africa."

But JM could never not get drunk and stoned and was too narcissistic to sacrifice the adulation.

JM was four-years-old when, on a road between Santa Fe and Albuquerque, his family witnessed a fatal truck wreck in which several Pueblo Indians were killed.

JM's naval officer father (who was employed at a New Mexico atomic site) appeared to do what he could to aid the Indians.

He made phone calls and arranged for an ambulance.

But as the Morrison family car was driving away from the wreck, four-year-old Jim was shrieking, as though in pain.

JM

That Indian's spirit passed into my body, man.

That fucking "spirit-transfer" was the most important thing that ever happened to me.

SPEAKER

When JM wasn't outright cruel or moodily disgusted, he was intellectually curious, reading odd books and having funky ideas--even for a white American coming of age in the hallucinogenic Sixties.

He read Antonin Artaud's *The Theater of Cruelty* which appeared to confirm and elaborate his sense of self.

Like Artaud, JM imagined he felt life too acutely to inhabit its lies, hence his "addiction" to violent extremes which toyed with madness.

With his need to secede from the world, reside—however transiently—in that suspended state induced by alcohol, drugs, radical performance, death, if it came to that.

Artaud's theater of cruelty advocated performative seismic-like shocks to plunge the audience into the chaos that constitutes the world, but which is officially obscured from sight?

Morrison's theatrical gyrations were familiar in rock performance, but he added a Kurt-Weil cabaret aspect which functioned potently in and out of Ray Manzarek's organ riffs.

JM's voice, though untrained, was a strong, supple baritone, and at his best his timing and musicality were close to impeccable.

(If these were the Cold War 50s, JM might have modeled himself after a crooner like Tony Martin rather than the abject Artaud).

Artaud had once been beautiful, but emotional torment, opium, and lengthy periods of institutionalization ravaged his body and spirit.

Was it Morrison's intention to invoke Artaud damn the consequence?

Like Lord Byron, the fated club-foot genius, JM had pouting lips, a weak chin, and was prone to corpulence.

Early in his career JM had to drop thirty pounds, from 160 to 130, to look svelte and justify his nom-de-theatre, the Lizard King.

Byron swam and fornicated to maintain his weight; he also vomited and took laxatives.

Coke and speed helped keep JM lean.

He fornicated, of course, when he wasn't limp from boozing, and he did a lot of sweating during performances.

It was a losing battle.

When he left for Paris in 1971, he was positively fat, with a massive, full bearded head.

It was rumored that once, Byron, drunk and in high dudgeon,displayed his penis in the House of Lords, then proceeded to urinate from a balcony onto the head of the Viscount something-or-other who had previously expressed an unflattering word about Byron's verses.

At an overflowing Miami concert, with as many as 13,000 fans, JM, drunk and stoned, obscenely mocked his audience for slavishly admiring his "sexual beauty" rather than actively "having a good time."

JM

Do you want to see my cock? Yeah or no?

Sounds like Yeah.

SPEAKER

Then he either undid his leather pants and displayed his penis, or faked doing it.

Witnesses' accounts varied.

The Sixties Zeitgeist was turning: JM was prosecuted for obscenity and sentenced to a prison term he never served.

QUESTION: Did JM, 27-years-old, in Paris, die in his bath of a myocardial infarction, as the official death certificate concluded?

Did he overdose on heroin, coke and alcohol?

Did he die elsewhere in Paris then was transported to his flat and set in the bath?

For mysterious French reasons, no autopsy was conducted. According to some reports, there was blood in the bathtub.

Was he murdered by his disturbed long-time companion Pamela Courson, who gave conflicting versions of JM's death?

Pamela Courson would herself die of a heroin overdose three years later.

Did the FBI or CIA assassinate the Lizard King to cast aspersions on the counterculture?

Evidently no one actually witnessed JM's corpse placed into the casket, which was then closed so that even his grieving parents were forbidden to view him.

Mourners observed that his gravesite in the Père Lachaise cemetery seemed much too small to contain an adult corpse.

Some mystics believe a gnome is buried in that plot. Jim Morrison, they insist, is still alive, swimming sidestroke in the Gulf of Aden while working part-time as a slave trader on the Horn of Africa?

DEATH IN TEXAS

PLAYERS

Texas death-row inmates (about to be executed)
Various

Someone, perhaps offstage, reads the brief details about each inmate. Then the inmate delivers his/her "last statement into the old microphone which faces the 'audience.'"

Other figures are semi-visible, such as the warden, prison guards, and in the "audience" behind the mesh fence, scattered members of the various families.

To the left are the outlines of the lethal injection execution chamber.

After each inmate speaks a guard escorts them to the execution chamber.

Then another inmate follows to the microphone.

Date of Execution: March 3, 2003

Offender: Marcus Cotton #999252

County: Cherokee

Last Statement:

Well Moms, sometime it works out like this.

Love life, live long.

When you dealin' wit' reality, real ain' always what you wan' it to be.

Take care yousefs.

Tell my kids I love 'em.

God is real. He is fixin' to find out some deep things that are real.

Bounce back, baby, you know what I'm sayin'.

Yawl take care yousefs.

That's it, Warden.

Date of Execution: July 28, 2005

Offender: Virgil Ravenfeather #921338

County: Navarro

Last Statement:

Only the sky and the green grass goes on forever and today is a good day to die.

Date of Execution: January 16, 2002

Offender: Horace Allen #987225

County: Liberty

Last Statement:

Members of Mrs. Lackey's family, like I said, I take responsibility for the death of your daughter in 1989.

I'm deeply sorry for the loss of your beloved daughter.

I am a human being also, I know how it feels.

I cannot explain and can't give you no answers.

I can give you just one thing.

I'm'a give a life for a life.

I am not saying this to be facetious.

I hope yawl find comfort in my execution.

As for me, I am happy, that is why you see me smiling.

I am glad to be leaving this world.

I am going to a better place.

I have made peace with God, I am born again.

I hope you get over any malice or hatred you feel.

God bless all yawl.

[Sings]

Amazing Grace, how sweet the sound,

That saved a wretch like me,

I once was lost but now am found,

Was blind, but now, I see . . .

Date of Execution: February 8, 2003

Offender: Octavio Guerra #978923

County: Zapata

Last Statement:

I want to thank my family for their help and moral support and their struggle.

Woulda been a whole lot harder without their love.

Me? I'm just going back home. I will see yawl one of these days.

Just don't rush it. I will be there always. I'll be watching over you.

I love yawl, huh.

I'll see yawl in Slayton, Texas.

Dios te mandas contigo mi espiritu.

Cuida mi familia.

Pull the plug, Warden.

Date of Execution: June 6, 2006

Offender: Timothy Tilton #906823

County: Red River

Last Statement:

I know you folks is here to find closure for the things I have done.

There are no words to describe the pain and suffering you have went through all these years, and that is something that I cannot take back from you.

I hope that Megan, if she is here present today, knows that today I hope you all get peace and joy.

I am sorry it has taken 14 years to get closure.

If it would have brung closure or brung her back, I would have did this years ago

I promise, I promise.

I didn't mean to inflict the pain and suffering on your family.

I pray that she is safe in heaven.

I pray that you find closure and strength.

I am sorry, I am truly sorry.

You all take care.

Pastor, tell Megan I am sorry.

Date of Execution: June 13, 2001

Offender: Johnny Saginaw #999222

County: San Jacinto

Last Statement:

I deeply regret what happened. I did not intentionally or knowingly harm anyone.

That's it and *didmau*. (Vietnamese for "let's get out of here.")

Date of Execution: May 24, 2006

Offender: Jesus Aguilar #911383

County: Gillespie

Last Statement:

I would like to say to my family, I am alright.

Leo? Donde esta, Leo?

Esta aqui, Leo?

Don't lie, man. Be happy.

Are you happy?

Are you all happy?

Date of Execution: September 27, 2004

Offender: Dwayne-Earl Clapp #999150

County: Scurry

Last Statement:

Sharla, Lamar, Sonny, Michelle, yawl know I love you.

Tell ever'body I said hey, I love 'em and I will see 'em on the other side. K?

Now I just pray that if there is anything 'gainst me--that God will take it on home.

I don't want nobody talkin' bad at nobody.

I don't want nobody bein' bitter.

Keep clean hearts and I will see yawl on the other side. K?

I love yawl, stay sweet.

Kick the tires and light the fire, I am goin' home to see my infant baby girl and my mom.

Date of Execution: August 14, 2002

Offender: Javier Suarez #944906

County: Palo Pinto

Last Statement:

First of all, I would like to apologize to the family members of the Cadena family for whatever hurt and suffering I caused you.

I hope you find it in your heart to forgive me.

The peace you find will be a temporary peace, true peace will come only through Jesus Christ.

I pray through this execution that you will find the peace you seek.

Give yourself to Jesus .

I thought about your loved one a whole lot.

He will be in heaven waitin' on me.

I will then talk to him personal and ask for his forgiveness

To my family, I thank you and love you for being there for me and supporting me.

Forgive me for the pain I caused you.

[Spanish]

To all the people of Méjico that supported me: I carry each and every one of you in my heart.

If you are going to demonstrate, I don't want you to do nothing crazy to these people.

They are good people, they have suffered enough.

Long live Méjico.

Date of Execution: May 28, 2002

Offender: Napoleon Beazley 111 #999141

County: Rockwall

Last Statement:

The act I committed to put me here was brutal and senseless.

But the person that committed that act is no longer here—I am.

I'm not going to struggle physically against these restraints.

I'm not going to shout, use profanity or make threats.

Understand though that I am saddened by what is happening here tonight.   I'm disappointed that a system supposed to protect and uphold what is just can be so

much like me when I made the same shameful mistake.

I'm sorry that John Luttig died.

And I'm sorry that it was something in me that caused all

of this to happen to begin with.

Tonight we tell the world that there are no second chances

in the eyes of justice.

Tonight we tell our children that in some instances killing

is righteous.

There are a lot of men like me on death row --good men--

who fell to the same misguided emotions.

Give those men a chance to do what's right, undo their wrongs.

A lot of them want to fix the mess they started, but

don't know how.

The problem is the system is telling them there is no

rehabilitation.

Only unforgiving punishment.

Date of Execution: September 11, 2001

Offender: Karla Faye Tucker #922923

County: Yuma

Last Statement:

I would like to say to the Mosebys that I am very, very sorry of depriving you of your mama and daddy.

To Warden Taggett and Chaplain Jesse Turner, I thank you very, very much, you been so good to me.

To my family and friends that has stuck by me, I love yawl from the bottom of my heart.

I am going to be face to face with Jesus now.

I will see all yawl when you get up there.

I will be dressed in wat."

Date of Execution: December 7, 2000

Offender: Claude Jones #980890

County: Nueces

Last Statement:

To your family, ah, I hope that this can bring some closure to yawl.

I am sorry for your loss and, hey, I love all yawl.

Let's go.

Date of Execution: May 17, 2006

Offender: Jermaine Herron #979210

County: Potter

Last Statement:

Mr. Jerry Nutt, I just hope this brings some kind of peace to your family.

I wish I could bring them back, but I cain't.

I hope my death brings peace to you all.

Don't hang on to the hate.

Mama, I love you.

Lord forgive me for my sins because here I come.

Date of Execution: May 28, 2002

Offender: Adolf Wolfli #999666

County: San Augustine

Last Statement:

You gentlemen and ladies of quality who frequently don't know yourselves what Christian virtue and justice are, look at the sunken, deep-set eyes of the lower classes, where you can see all too clearly the sorrow and misery that weigh on their hearts.

Not everyone who sees his grieved and martyred face in

the washroom mirror in the morning is a murderer or drug

addict.

On the contrary, the grounds for his misery are to be

sought elsewhere.

You friends near and far.

If among you there is anyone without sin, let him come to

me, and I will implore him for compassion and mercy.

Date of Execution: April 20, 2005

Offender: Troy Kunkle #954811

County: Angelina

Last Statement:

I've been hanging around this popsicle stand way too long.

Before I leave, I want to tell you all.

Bury me deep, lay two speakers at my feet, put

headphones on my skull and rock and roll me when I'm dead.

I'll see you all in hell.

Date of Execution: August 23, 2005

Offender: Jimmy Blackmon #924591

County: Hunt

Last Statement:

(This offender declined to make a final statement.)

About the Author

Harold Jaffe is the author of 30 novels, short fiction collections, essays, and plays. His recent books include *Porn-anti-Porn* and *BRUT: Writings on Art & Artists*.

Jaffe is editor-in-chief of *Fiction International.*

MASKS Alphonse Allais

NO BILE! Alphonse Allais
CAPTAIN CAP Alphonse Allais

DOUBLE OVER Alphonse Allais
THE ALPHONSE ALLAIS READER
THE ZOMBIE OF GREAT PERU Pierre-Corneille de Blessebois

SMELLS LIKE TEEN 'PATAPHYSICS Norman Conquest
LE CHAT NOIR EXPOSED Caroline Crépiat

COLLECTED MONOLOGUES Charles Cros
UPSIDE-DOWN STORIES Charles Cros
ANGEL OF EVERYTHING Catherine D'Avis
TODAY IS THE DAY THAT WILL MATTER Debra Di Blasi
FROM THEIR LIPS TO HIS EARS Denis Diderot
EVE'S ACADEMY Eurydice
THE PISSERS' THEATRE Eckhard Gerdes

WEIRDLY OUT WEST Rhys Hughes
THE POPE'S MUSTARD-MAKER Alfred Jarry
ESCAPE ARTISTS Sue Orwell
HERE LIES MEMORY Doug Rice
JANEY QUIXOTE Doug Rice
CLOCKS Jason E. Rolfe
RETALIATION Marquis de Sade
SHORTEN THE CLASSICS Doug Skinner
THE UNKNOWN ADJECTIVE Doug Skinner
CRITICS & MY TALKING DOG Stefan Themerson

TOURIST: A NOVEL Temenuga Trifonova
THE NEW URGE READER 4 Various

LE SCAT NOIR ENCYCLOPÉDIE Various
THE BEST OF LE SCAT NOIR Various

OULIPO PORNOBONGO ANTHOLOGY Various
A DIRTY STORY AS YOU LIKE IT Kim Vodicka

APRIL FIREBALL: EARLY STORIES Tom Whalen
THREE PLAYS BY D. HARLAN WILSON

VAHAZAR Witkacy

www.ingramcontent.com/pod-product-compliance
Lightning Source LLC
Chambersburg PA
CBHW020625250626
47154CB00004B/1673